Angela Bowling took her shopping bag and
set off for the village. It was a bright spring
morning, but the wind had blown all night
in the great woods and there were leaves
and fallen branches everywhere.
And there was something else . . .

'My goodness,' said Angela. 'It's a baby bird blown out of his nest. He needs someone to look after him.'

20091540

Quentin Blake

Loveykins

A Tom Maschler Book

JONATHAN CAPE

LONDON

For the angels of "Le Cayenne"
with love as always

She wrapped him up carefully in her scarf,
and off home they went.

When they got there she added a shawl and an old cardigan so that the little bird was warm and safe. Then she sat him in a decorative basket that once used to hold flowers.

She fed him with spoonfuls of warm milk.
'He must have a name,' said Angela.
'I shall call him Augustus.'

Only the best was good enough for Augustus.

She fed him on
creamed carrots,

chocolate éclairs,

Black Forest gâteau,

and boxes of chocolates with assorted centres.

Augustus ate the whole lot.
'Who's a loveykins, then?' said Angela.

Next morning Angela bought a smart new
pushchair. It had a special umbrella to keep
off the rain and the sun.
Every morning after that Angela would wrap
Augustus up carefully so that he didn't catch
cold, and they would set off to the village.

They met Elsie Lyons and the twins by
the duck pond . . .

Miss Twyford and her dollies
in the High Street . . .

and Harold and his brother Gerald with
their dog Wellington outside the library.

At the village store Angela Bowling bought
all the best things to eat she could find.

Augustus ate and ate
and as the days went
by he grew bigger
and bigger.

At last he was too big
for his basket, and too
big for the pushchair,
especially with all
those cardigans
and eiderdowns
wrapped round
him to make
sure he didn't
catch cold.

So Angela Bowling bought a brand new
garden shed especially for Augustus.
Every morning she would take him a tray
of good things to eat.

And then once again there came a night
of dreadful weather, and huge gales blew
through the great woods.

In the morning Angela Bowling got up, put on her dressing gown, and stepped out to see how her little loveykins had spent the night. But what did she see before her?

The garden shed had been blown flat by the gales, and there, with eiderdowns and cardigans strewn about him, stood Augustus, shaking his wings.

Angela Bowling
fainted clean away.

Augustus covered her
over safely with a pink
flowery eiderdown.

Then, his wings creaking slightly
with lack of use, he began to fly.

He flew through the village, over
    Elsie Lyons and the twins . . .

over Miss Twyford and
    her dollies . . .

and over Harold and his
brother Gerald and
their dog Wellington.

He flew up into the trees of the great woods.
There he ate several beetles and the remains
of a dead squirrel.

And then he flew on up,
up into the bright sky.

Further and further he rose, circling on the warm winds high above the clouds.

Far below he could see Angela Bowling
sleeping peacefully under the pink flowery
eiderdown, and stretched out before him –

such prospects!

such vistas!

It took Angela Bowling a long time to recover from her shock, but after six months she had her garden shed rebuilt. In it she started a wonderful collection of cactuses of all shapes and sizes.

And every so often, just when she is least expecting it, there is a rustle of wings and Augustus is there on the roof of the shed. He brings her a present: a dead mouse, perhaps, or a few beetles.

She never eats them.

LOVEYKINS
A JONATHAN CAPE BOOK: 0 224 06471 1

Published in Great Britain by Jonathan Cape,
an imprint of Random House Children's Books

This edition published 2002

1 3 5 7 9 10 8 6 4 2

RANDOM HOUSE CHILDREN'S BOOKS
61-63 Uxbridge Rd, London W5 5SA
A division of The Random House Group Ltd
RANDOM HOUSE AUSTRALIA (PTY) LTD
20 Alfred Street, Milsons Point, Sydney,
New South Wales 2061, Australia
RANDOM HOUSE NEW ZEALAND LTD
18 Poland Road, Glenfield, Auckland 10, New Zealand
RANDOM HOUSE (PTY) LTD
Endulini, 5A Jubilee Road, Parktown 2193, South Africa

THE RANDOM HOUSE GROUP Limited Reg. No. 954009
www.**kids**at**randomhouse**.co.uk

A CIP catalogue record for this book is available from the British Library

Printed in Singapore by Tien Wah Press